~ Christmas 2001 ~

~ for our nephew Brooks,
as he begins to
learn about the world
the things in ~

~ with love ~
Aunt Lynn & Uncle Danny

All the Way to Morning

by Marc Harshman

illustrated by Felipe Dávalos

Marshall Cavendish   New York

Text copyright © 1999 by Marc Harshman
Illustrations copyright © 1999 by Felipe Dávalos
All rights reserved
Marshall Cavendish, 99 White Plains Road, Tarrytown, New York
The text of this book is set in 18 point Meridien Medium.
The illustrations are rendered in acrylics.

Library of Congress Cataloging-in-Publication Data.
Harshman, Marc.
All the way to morning / by Marc Harshman ; illustrated by Felipe Dávalos.
p.   cm.
Summary: Children around the world hear different night sounds before they go to sleep.
ISBN 0-7614-5042-4
[1. Bedtime—Fiction. 2. Night—Fiction. 3. Sleep—Fiction. 4. Sound—Fiction.] I. Dávalos, Felipe, ill. II. Title.
PZ7.H256247Al   1999   [E] — dc21   98-28177   CIP   AC

Printed in Italy
First Edition

1   3   5   6   4   2

For Gillian "Emiko" and her brother, Jesse —*M. H.*

The campfire burns low.
The moon swims above the pines.
I crawl into my sleeping bag
and listen to the katydids
signing their night songs.

Dad tells me:
"As earth
turns day
into night
kids just like you
get ready to sleep
and listen, too."

"What do they hear?" I ask.

Meli hears the fruit bats
squeak, squeak, squeaking
as they swoop through the dark,
feeding in the air.

Western Samoa

Emiko hears the stream
rushing, rushing, rushing
down the falls
through the tea grove
all the way to the sea.

Japan

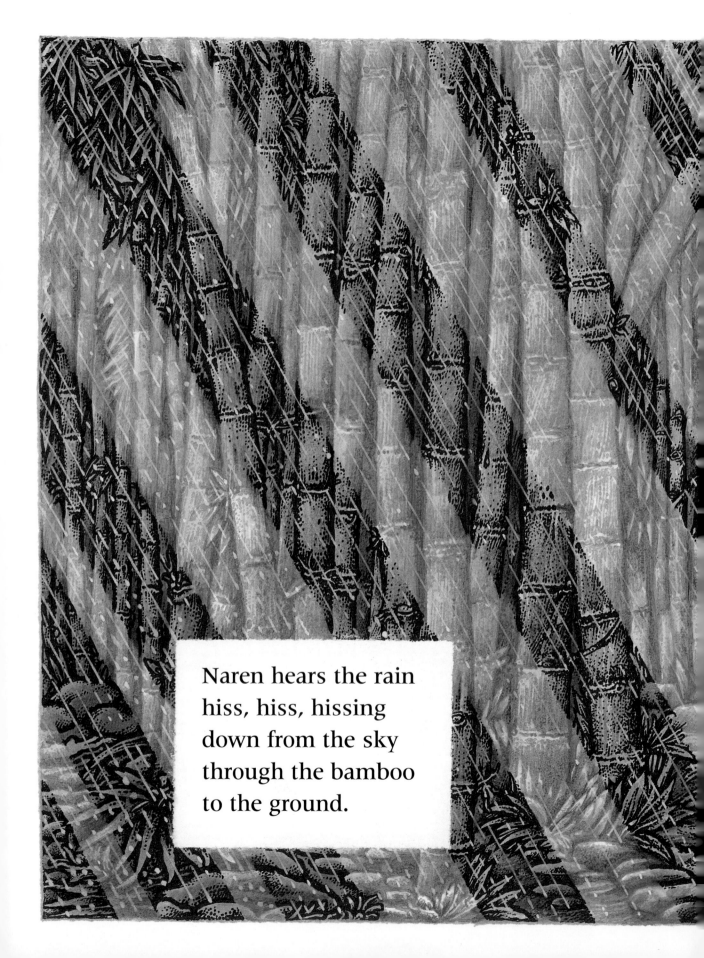

Naren hears the rain
hiss, hiss, hissing
down from the sky
through the bamboo
to the ground.

Kampuchea

Rama hears the train's
rick-a-rack, rick-a-rack
down the tracks
toward faraway Bombay.

India

Lekeni hears the jackal
yip, yip, yipping
out among the thorn trees
searching for food.

Kenya

Moshe hears a hammer
ping, ping, pinging
in the coppersmith's yard
where the fig trees grow.

Israel

Habib hears the sand
sift, sift, sifting,
streaming with the wind
across the open desert.

Egypt

Armand hears a violin
singing, singing, singing
down the hall
where Father plays
in the kitchen.

Italy

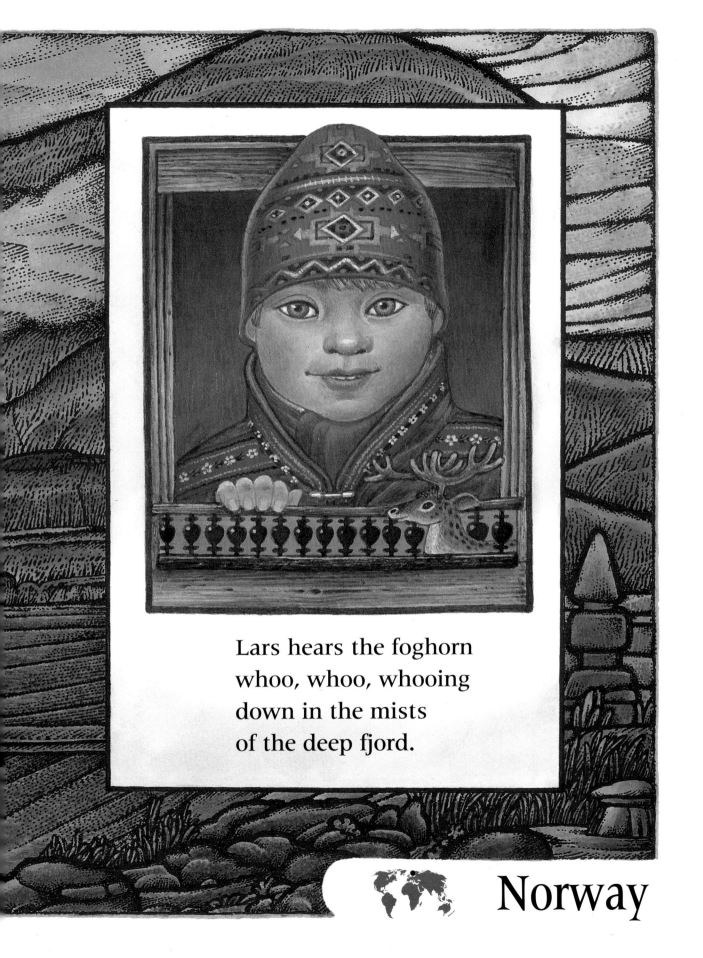

Lars hears the foghorn
whoo, whoo, whooing
down in the mists
of the deep fjord.

Norway

Fiona hears the waves
lap, lap, lapping
along the shore
and clear across the loch.

Scotland

Maria hears the monkeys
howling, howling, howling
deep in the jungle
high up in the trees.

Brazil

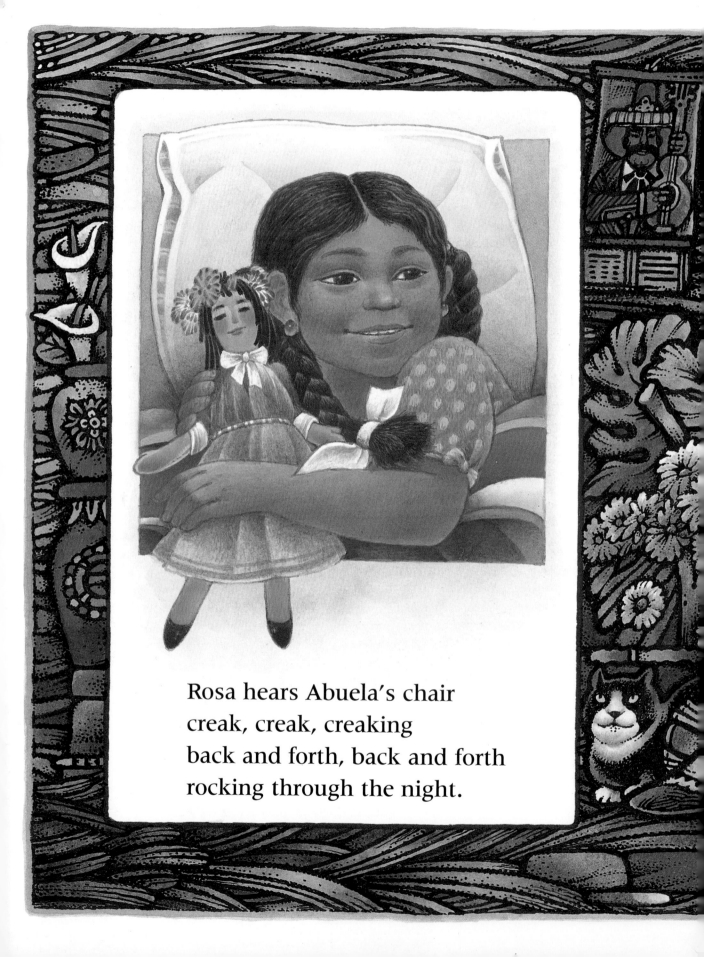

Rosa hears Abuela's chair
creak, creak, creaking
back and forth, back and forth
rocking through the night.

Mexico

Willy hears the dogs
bark, bark, barking
down in the alley
below the silvery buildings.

USA

"And now,"
Dad says,
"we will listen, too.
Listen for sleep."

I do as he says.
I listen
and imagine all the friends
I've never met
listening, too,
just like me
all over the world
listening and dreaming

all the way to morning.